Just One More Story

by **Jennifer Brutschy**

illustrated by **Cat Bowman Smith**

Orchard Books • New York
An Imprint of Scholastic Inc.

Printed in Singapore   46
Book design by Nancy Goldenberg
The text of this book is set in 14 point Plantin.
The illustrations are watercolor.
1 3 5 7 9 10 8 6 4 2   02 03 04 05

Library of Congress Cataloging-in-Publication Data
Brutschy, Jennifer.
Just one more story / Jennifer Brutschy ; illustrated by Cat Bowman Smith.
p.   cm.
Summary: Austin and his parents travel around the country in their trailer performing with
their band, and every night Austin's father tells him one bedtime story, until the night they
stay in a two-story house instead of their trailer.
ISBN 0-439-31767-3 (alk. paper)
[1. Story-telling—Fiction.] I. Smith, Cat Bowman, ill. II. Title.
PZ7.B8288 Ju 2002 [E]—dc21   99-58610

With love to Mom and Dad
for filling my childhood
with books and stories
—*J.B.*

To Jacob Bowman Sciandra,
who also loves
just one more story
—*C.B.S.*

Austin and his family were on the road. They called themselves
The Swamp Snakes. Dad played the fiddle, Mom sang
country-western, and Austin banged the tambourine.

Every day was a different crowd. Every week was a different town.
But every night in their trailer was exactly the same.

Austin got a drink in his dinosaur mug. He lined his stuffed animals at the foot of the bed, pulled up his quilt, and called out, "Story time!"

Every night Dad told a story and tucked the quilt under Austin's chin.

"Just one more story?" Austin always begged.

"You know the rules, cowboy," Dad said. "Just one story at bedtime."
Then he kissed Austin on the forehead, snapped off the light, and said,
"Don't let the rattlers nibble at your toes."

Austin fell asleep while Mom and Dad whispered softly nearby.

One Texas night they played Hank's Music Hall.
They set the room to rocking and the cowboy boots to stomping.
"Yippee!" cried Austin.

But when the show was over and the crowd had gone home, his
bed felt as snug as a grizzly bear's cave.

"Just one more story?" he asked sleepily.

"You know the rules," Dad said, and he kissed him good-night.

It was the same every night and in every town till they pulled into
Tuscaloosa, Alabama.

"Let's pop in on Uncle Roy," Dad said.

Mom smiled. "It'll do us good to stretch out in a real house."

That evening both families danced and fiddled and sang until their yawns made more noise than their music.

"Such a nice settling-down place," Mom said. "I wish a two-story house were in the cards for me."

"Two stories?" Austin asked.

"Yup," said Dad. "Now let's head up those stairs for some shut-eye."

Austin had to have his drink in a paper cup. He had to snuggle under scratchy blankets instead of his fluffy quilt. But he was ready for those stories.

"I'm all tuckered out," Dad said, "but I think I can manage
a story."

"*Two* stories," demanded Austin.

"Hey, you know the rules," said Dad. "Just one story at bedtime."

"But," said Austin, "this is a *two*-story house."

Dad's face lost all its tired creases. "Not *that* kind of story," he said.
"Two stories means two floors. One upstairs and one downstairs."
"Oh," said Austin.

"All right, cowboy," Dad agreed. "Two stories for a two-story house."
And he told "The Roly-Poly Rice Ball" and one about Anansi.

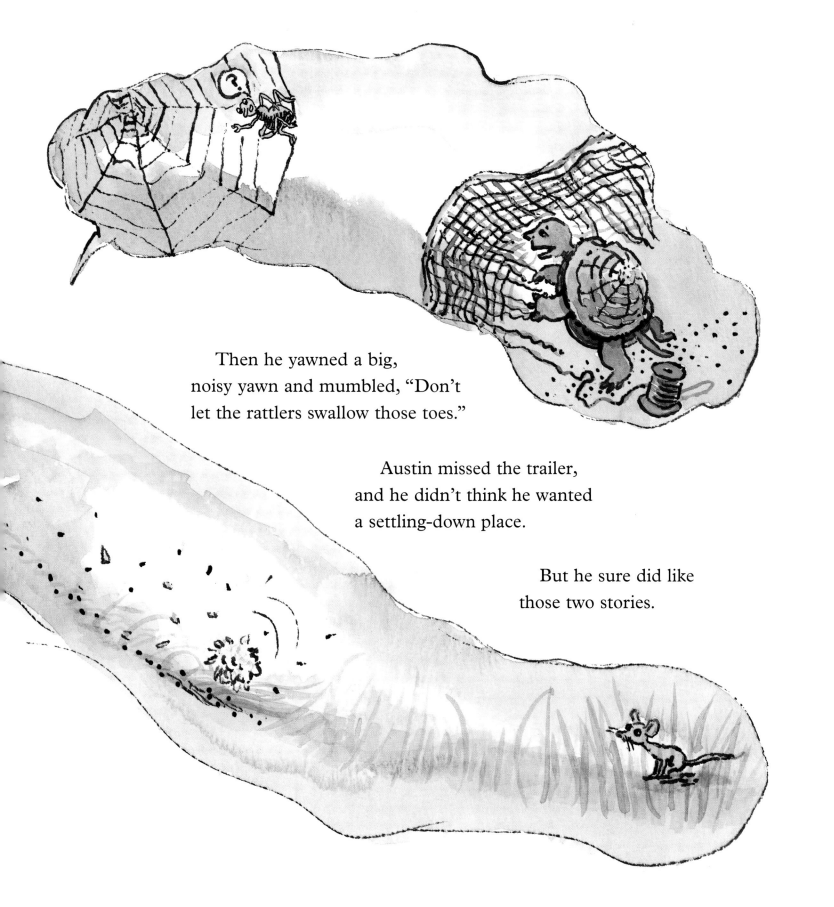

Then he yawned a big,
noisy yawn and mumbled, "Don't
let the rattlers swallow those toes."

Austin missed the trailer,
and he didn't think he wanted
a settling-down place.

But he sure did like
those two stories.

The next morning they hit the road. By suppertime they were tuning up at Charlie's Corner.

"Ladies and gentlemen!" said Charlie. "Introducing . . .
The Swamp Snakes!"
They played through supper, with everybody twirling their
partners on the dance-hall floor.

Later that night they were back in the trailer, cozy as a family of mice. Austin got a drink in his dinosaur mug, lined up his animals, and called out, "Story time!"

"Just one story tonight," Dad said, and he told about the knee-high man in the gooey, gooey swamp.

"I liked *two* stories better," Austin complained as Dad pulled up his comfy quilt.

"You and me both," muttered Mom, trying to find room
for her toe kicks.

Austin winked at Dad. "Not *that* kind of story," he said.
Dad winked back and kissed Austin on the forehead. "Watch
out for those yellow-bellied rattlers," he said.

In Louisiana Dad won a whole mess of money in a fiddling contest.
"Let's splurge," Mom said.

The next night they rolled into San Antonio. Austin was half asleep by the time they stopped at a towering hotel. He didn't notice the glass chandeliers. He didn't see the fish tank in the lobby. He hardly even knew that Dad was nudging him into an elevator and pushing a button.

"Drat," said Dad, when it didn't light up. "It's busted.
I can't walk up eleven stories."

"ELEVEN STORIES!" Austin shouted, suddenly awake.

"No!" said Dad. "That doesn't mean . . ."

A few minutes later Austin was in bed, and Dad began his stories:
"Down by the crick there lived a one-eyed cowboy. . . ."

Austin snuggled in. He didn't like the hotel bed as much as his own bed. And he missed his dinosaur mug.

But he sure did like those eleven stories.